BATTLETECH™
ACTIVITY BOOK

COLORING · PUZZLES
MAZES · CODES · MORE!

NO GUTS, NO GALAXY!

BattleTech is a science-fiction "space opera" set in the factional, militarized universe of the thirty-first century. Humanity has spread to the stars and spawned titanic interstellar empires, each controlling hundreds of worlds across a combined region of space stretching more than a thousand light years.

Following the rise of the six Great Noble Houses, a mighty Star League was forged, heralding a golden age of prosperity.

However, treachery undermined the Star League and led to the murder of the First Lord and the fall of House Cameron. The rulers of the remaining five Great Houses each proclaimed themselves the new First Lord of the crumbling Star League, and thus began the Succession Wars.

For twelve generations, armies of BattleMechs clashed across more than 2,000 colonized planets of the Inner Sphere, visiting such destruction on humanity's technological capabilities that old, scavenged 'Mechs often outperformed newly built models. But the landscape is changing, and fierce new enemies from beyond the Periphery known as the Clans have thrown the Inner Sphere into chaos.

The year is 3050, and the fires of the Fourth Succession War have given way to new alliances in the face of this dire threat looming over the entire Inner Sphere. All five Houses desperately seek a way to turn back these invaders while continuing their technological renaissance.

Clan MechWarriors, whether newly graduated into the warrior caste or honed by decades of vicious combat, are hell-bent on conquering the Inner Sphere. The Great Houses and the skilled mercenaries at their command must work together against the Clans to snatch victory from the jaws of certain defeat.

THIS is BattleTech.

MECHWARRIORS

As soon as the first BattleMechs dominated the battlefields of the twenty-fifth century, the humans that piloted these awesome machines gained a power and influence well beyond what other soldiers on the field could command. An entire social class soon formed around those who piloted these increasingly important war machines. These so-called MechWarriors, the modern incarnation of knights, were given the monumental task of defending their homelands and their rulers. As with the Middle Ages of Europe, these MechWarriors were given honors in exchange for service. Some even received royal titles, conveying authority over entire worlds. Such honors usually had the direct effect of instilling utter loyalty toward whoever bestowed them.

BattleMechs have waxed and waned in rarity and numbers as the technology and production infrastructure to build and maintain them suffered during centuries of extended warfare.

During those eras when BattleMechs transitioned into rare commodities, many became owned by the MechWarriors who pilot them, with many 'Mechs having been passed down to a MechWarrior from their parents or relatives. Competitions within such families to see who will gain the right to become the next generation's MechWarrior—and thus the effective leader of that family—are fierce and brutal, with siblings taking sides and asking for no quarter.

BattleMechs that are not passed down are typically the property of the military, in which they serve with MechWarriors filling a roster slot in the military—or mercenary—force's structure.

BATTLEMECHS

—Excerpts from a promotional pamphlet originally distributed by Defiance Industries of Hesperus, Lyran Commonwealth, 3007

- *Standing from seven to sixteen meters tall, and weighing from twenty to one hundred tons*
- *Powered by an armored and shielded fusion reactor*
- *Skeleton of honeycombed, foamed aluminum core wrapped with stressed silicon carbide mono-filament and sheathed by a rigid, titanium-steel shell*
- *Locomotion generated via bundles of polyacetylene-fiber myomer muscles*
- *Protected by aligned-crystal steel over a layer of boron nitride impregnated with diamond monofilaments*
- *Mounting a swath of powerful weapons from charged particle beams to lasers, missiles to rapid-fire autocannons*
- *All at the command of the noble elite, the MechWarriors*

The modern BattleMech is the end result of more than 3,000 years of battlefield technology development. Combining awesome destructive power and unparalleled maneuverability, the BattleMech is perhaps the most complex machine ever produced. The undisputed master of thirty-first century warfare, the BattleMech seems destined to reign supreme for centuries to come.

LCT-1V LOCUST

ACS

CLASS: Light BattleMech

MASS: 20 tons

SPEED: 129 kph

JUMP JETS: None

ARMOR: 4 tons StarSlab/1

ARMAMENT: 1 Martell Medium Laser
2 SperryBrowning Machine Guns

SHD-2H SHADOW HAWK

CLASS: Medium BattleMech

MASS: 55 tons

SPEED: 86 kph

JUMP JETS: Pitban LFT-50 (90 m)

ARMOR: 9.5 tons Maximillian 43

ARMAMENT: 1 Armstrong J11 Autocannon

1 Holly Long Range Missile 5 Rack

1 Holly Short Range 2 Rack

1 Martell Model 5 Medium Laser

GRENDEL

PLOG19

CLASS: Medium Clan OmniMech
MASS: 45 tons
SPEED: 118 kph
JUMP JETS: Clan Standard 14X Series (210 m)

ARMOR: 7.5 tons Arcadia Compound
Delta VII Ferro-Fibrous
ARMAMENT: 1 ER Large Laser
3 ER Medium Lasers
1 ER Small Laser
1 Streak SRM-6

WSP-1A WASP

CLASS: Light BattleMech
MASS: 20 tons
SPEED: 97 kph
JUMP JETS: Rawlings 52 (180 m)

ARMOR: 3 tons Durallex Light
ARMAMENT: 1 Diverse Optics Type 2 Medium Laser
1 Bical SRM Twin-Rack

GRF-1N GRIFFIN

CLASS: Medium BattleMech

MASS: 55 tons

SPEED: 86 kph

JUMP JETS: Rawlings 55 (150 m)

ARMOR: 9.5 tons Starshield A

ARMAMENT: 1 Fusigon Particle Projection Cannon

1 Delta Dart Long Range Missile 10-Rack

CODE BREAKING

ComStar Adept Sandor Kalman has intercepted coded transmissions!
He's provided you with decoding ciphers—see if you can learn what the secret messages say.

ADDER (PUMA)

CLASS: Light Clan OmniMech

MASS: 35 tons

SPEED: 97 kph

JUMP JETS: None

ARMOR: 6 tons Star Lite Ferro-Fibrous

ARMAMENT: 1 Flamer

2 ER PPCs

PXH-1 PHOENIX HAWK

PLOG19

CLASS: Medium BattleMech

MASS: 45 tons

SPEED: 97 kph

JUMP JETS: Rawlings 45 (180 m)

ARMOR: 8 tons Durallex Light

ARMAMENT: 1 Harmon Large Laser
2 Harmon Medium Lasers
2 M100 Machine Guns

SHADOW CAT

CLASS: Medium Clan OmniMech

MASS: 45 tons

SPEED: 129 kph (with MASC)

JUMP JETS: Model KY Boosters (180 m)

ARMOR: 7 tons Compound H17 Ferro-Fibrous

ARMAMENT: 1 Gauss Rifle

2 ER Medium Lasers

Active Probe

RFL-3N RIFLEMAN

CLASS: Heavy BattleMech
MASS: 60 tons
SPEED: 64 kph
JUMP JETS: None

ARMOR: 7.5 tons Kallon Royalstar
ARMAMENT: 2 Magna Mk III Large Lasers
2 Magna Mk II Medium Lasers
2 Imperator-A Autocannons

CAN YOU IDENTIFY THESE 'MECH SILHOUETTES?

A: _____

B: _____

C: _____

D: _____

E: _____

F: _____

G: _____

H: _____

I: _____

OTT-7J OSTSCOUT

CLASS: Light BattleMech
MASS: 35 tons
SPEED: 129 kph

JUMP JETS: Ostmann Sct-A (240 m)
ARMOR: 4.5 tons Durallex Light
ARMAMENT: 1 Tronel II Medium Laser

BLR-1G BATTLEMASTER

CLASS: Assault BattleMech

MASS: 85 tons

SPEED: 64 kph

JUMP JETS: None

ARMOR: 14.5 tons StarGuard IV

ARMAMENT: 1 Donal Particle Projection Cannon

6 Martell Medium Lasers

2 SperryBrowning Machine Guns

1 Holly Short Range Missile 6 Pack

TDR-5S THUNDERBOLT

CLASS: Heavy BattleMech

MASS: 65 tons

SPEED: 64 kph

JUMP JETS: None

ARMOR: 13 tons Ryerson 150

ARMAMENT: 1 Sunglow Type 2 Large Laser

1 Delta Dart Long Range Missile 15-Rack

3 Diverse Optics Type 18 Medium Lasers

1 Bical Short Range Missile Twin-Rack

2 Voelkers 200 Machine Guns

MIST LYNX (KOSHI)

PLOG19

CLASS: Light Clan OmniMech

MASS: 25 tons

SPEED: 119 kph

JUMP JETS: Clan Light Series Mk I (180 m)

ARMOR: 3.5 tons Compound H17 Ferro-Fibrous

ARMAMENT: 1 Active Probe

1 LRM-10

1 Streak SRM-4

2 Machine Guns

STORMCROW (RYOKEN)

CLASS: Medium Clan OmniMech
MASS: 55 tons
SPEED: 97 kph
JUMP JETS: None

ARMOR: 9.5 tons Compound H17/2 Ferro-Fibrous
ARMAMENT: 3 ER Medium Lasers
2 ER Large Lasers

CLAN INSIGNIAS

Clan Ghost Bear

Clan Smoke Jaguar

Clan Jade Falcon

Clan Wolf

GREAT HOUSE INSIGNIAS

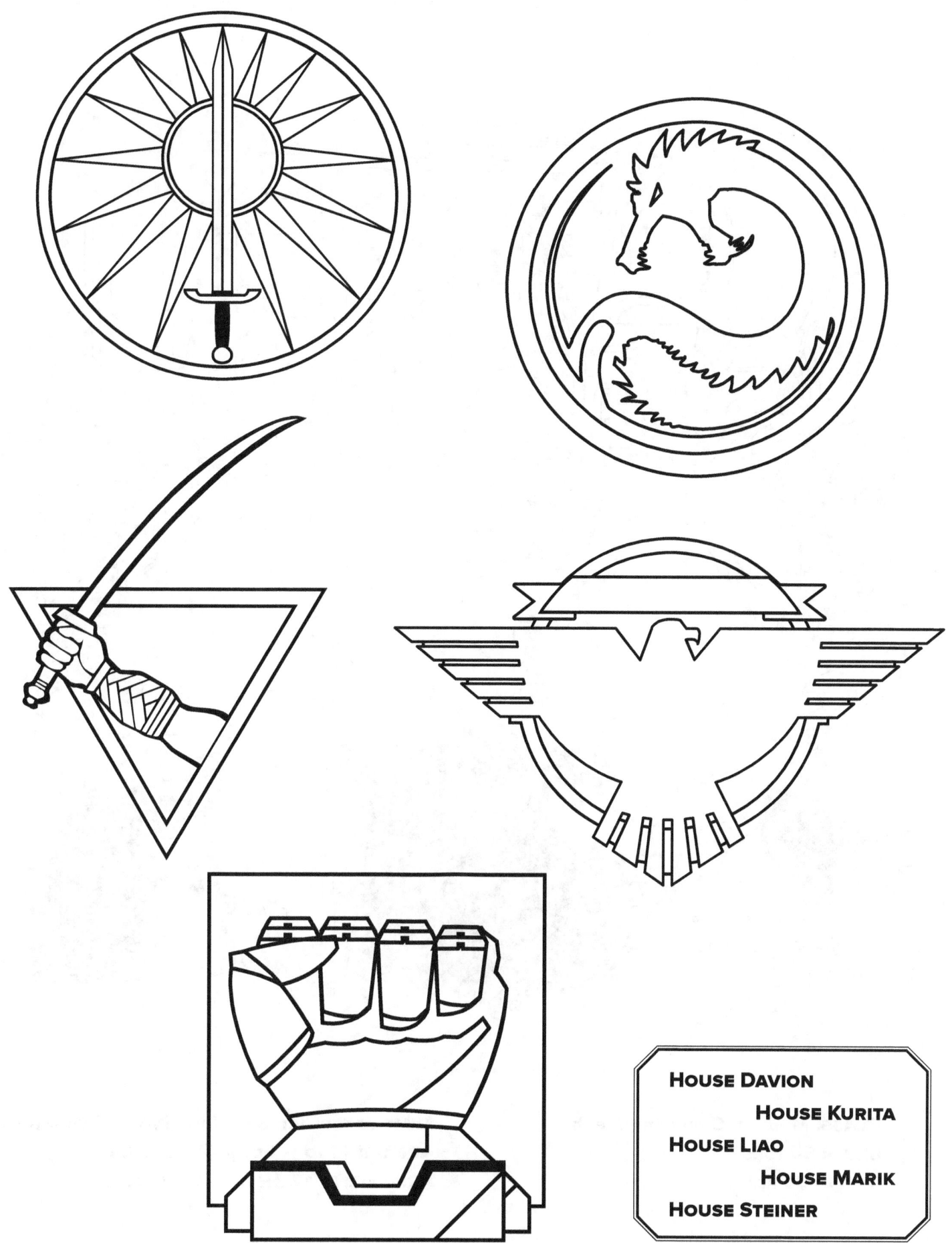

HOUSE DAVION

HOUSE KURITA

HOUSE LIAO

HOUSE MARIK

HOUSE STEINER

NOVA (BLACK HAWK)

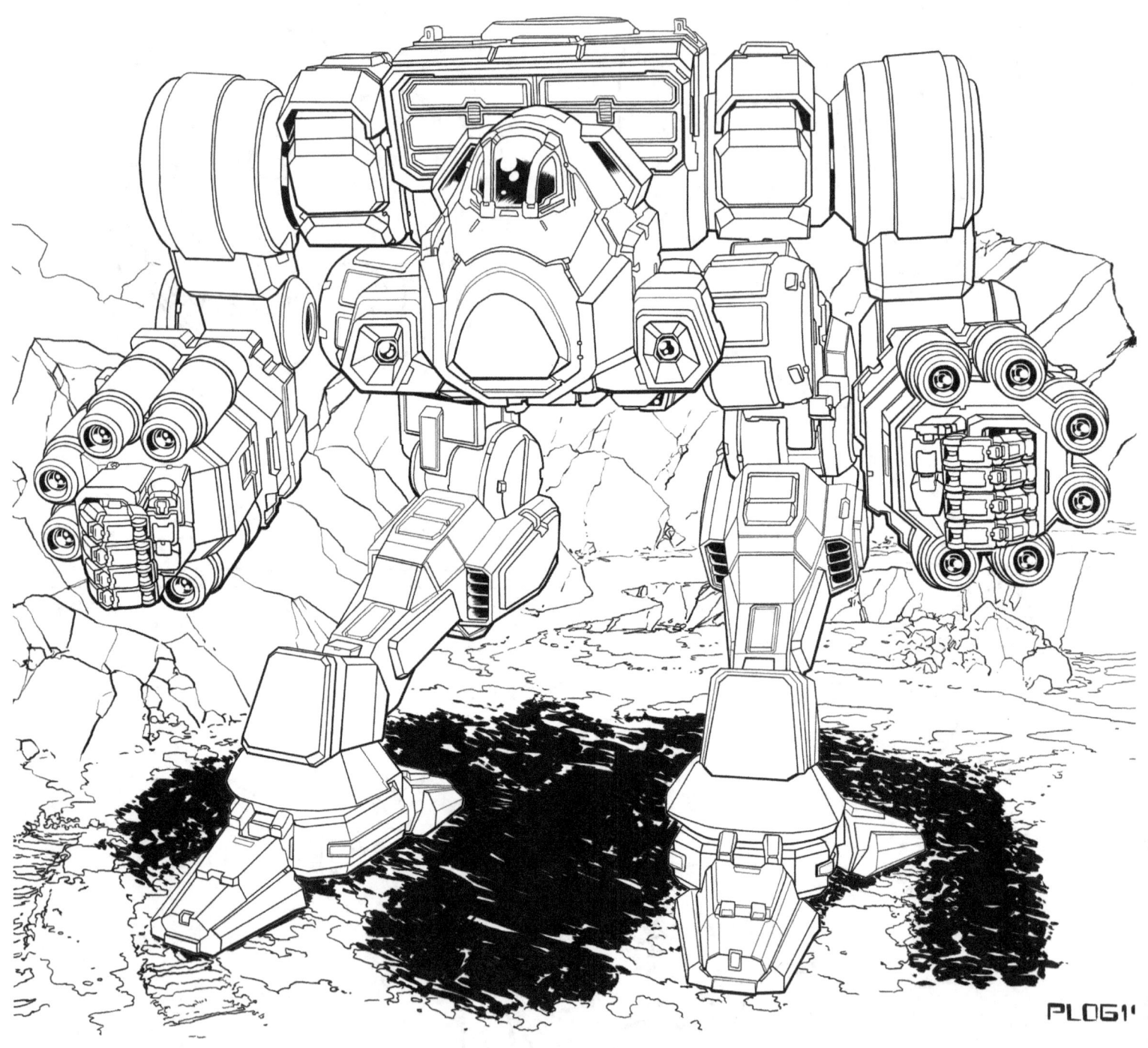

CLASS: Medium Clan OmniMech
MASS: 50 tons
SPEED: 86 kph

JUMP JETS: Clan Standard Type A2 (150 m)
ARMOR: 10 tons Forge Type HH30
ARMAMENT: 12 ER Medium Lasers

WORD SEARCH

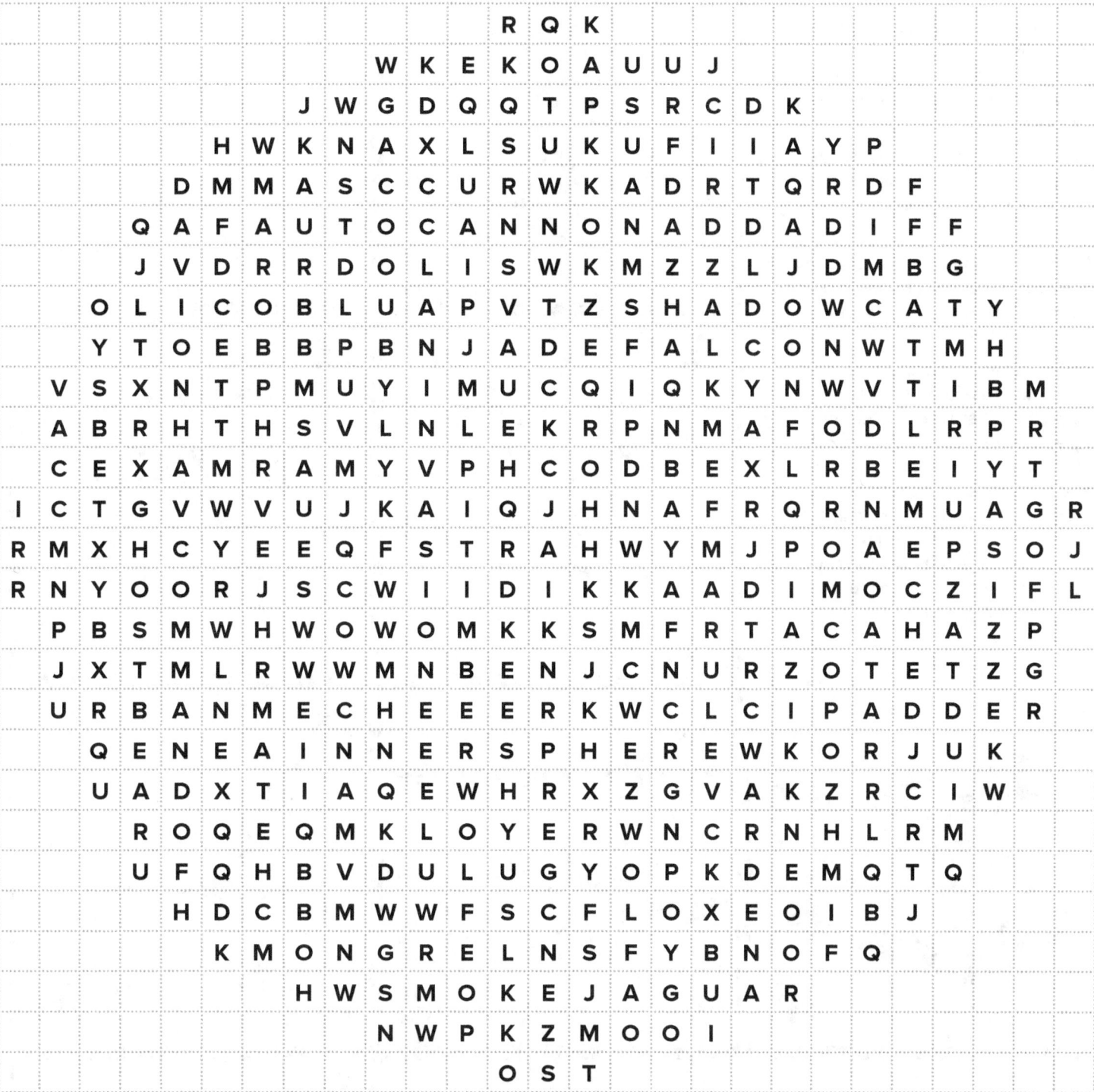

```
                  R Q K
                W K E K O A U U J
              J W G D Q Q T P S R C D K
            H W K N A X L S U K U F I I A Y P
            D M M A S C C U R W K A D R T Q R D F
          Q A F A U T O C A N N O N A D D A D I F F
          J V D R R D O L I S W K M Z Z L J D M B G
        O L I C O B L U A P V T Z S H A D O W C A T Y
        Y T O E B B P B N J A D E F A L C O N W T M H
    V S X N T P M U Y I M U C Q I Q K Y N W V T I B M
    A B R H T H S V L N L E K R P N M A F O D L R P R
    C E X A M R A M Y V P H C O D B E X L R B E I Y T
  I C T G V W V U J K A I Q J H N A F R Q R N M U A G R
  R M X H C Y E E Q F S T R A H W Y M J P O A E P S O J
  R N Y O O R J S C W I I D I K K A A D I M O C Z I F L
  P B S M W H W O W O M K K S M F R T A C A H A Z P
  J X T M L R W W M N B E N J C N U R Z O T E T Z G
  U R B A N M E C H E E E R K W C L C I P A D D E R
    Q E N E A I N N E R S P H E R E W K O R J U K
    U A D X T I A Q E W H R X Z G V A K Z R C I W
      R O Q E Q M K L O Y E R W N C R N H L R M
      U F Q H B V D U L U G Y O P K D E M Q T Q
        H D C B M W W F S C F L O X E O I B J
        K M O N G R E L N S F Y B N O F Q
          H W S M O K E J A G U A R
            N W P K Z M O O I
                O S T
```

ADDER	GHOST BEAR	MECHWARRIOR
AUTOCANNON	INNER SPHERE	MONGREL
AWESOME	JADE FALCON	SHADOW CAT
BATTLEMECH	KERENSKY	SMOKE JAGUAR
CLAN INVASION	KURITA	STEINER
COMMANDO	LIAO	TIMBER WOLF
CRUSADER	LOCUST	URBANMECH
DAVION	LRM	WARDEN
EXECUTIONER	MARIK	WOLF

DEAL-A-BATTLE

Cut out this page and the next (or copy or print them out) and cut out the twenty-two framed cards. (Multiple copies can be added to your deck as well.)

Shuffle the cards together and deal, face down, an equal number to yourself and your opponent (eleven cards each).

Take turns flipping over your top card and compare the digits to see who has the higher number—that player wins that card battle!

The victor of each card battle sets aside both cards (for ties, keep flipping until there is a winner; they keep all of those fought-over cards). Once all have been flipped, the owner of the most cards wins the war! If there's still a tie, players can play again to determine the ultimate power in the Inner Sphere! (Or tally up all the points each player collected and the higher score wins.)

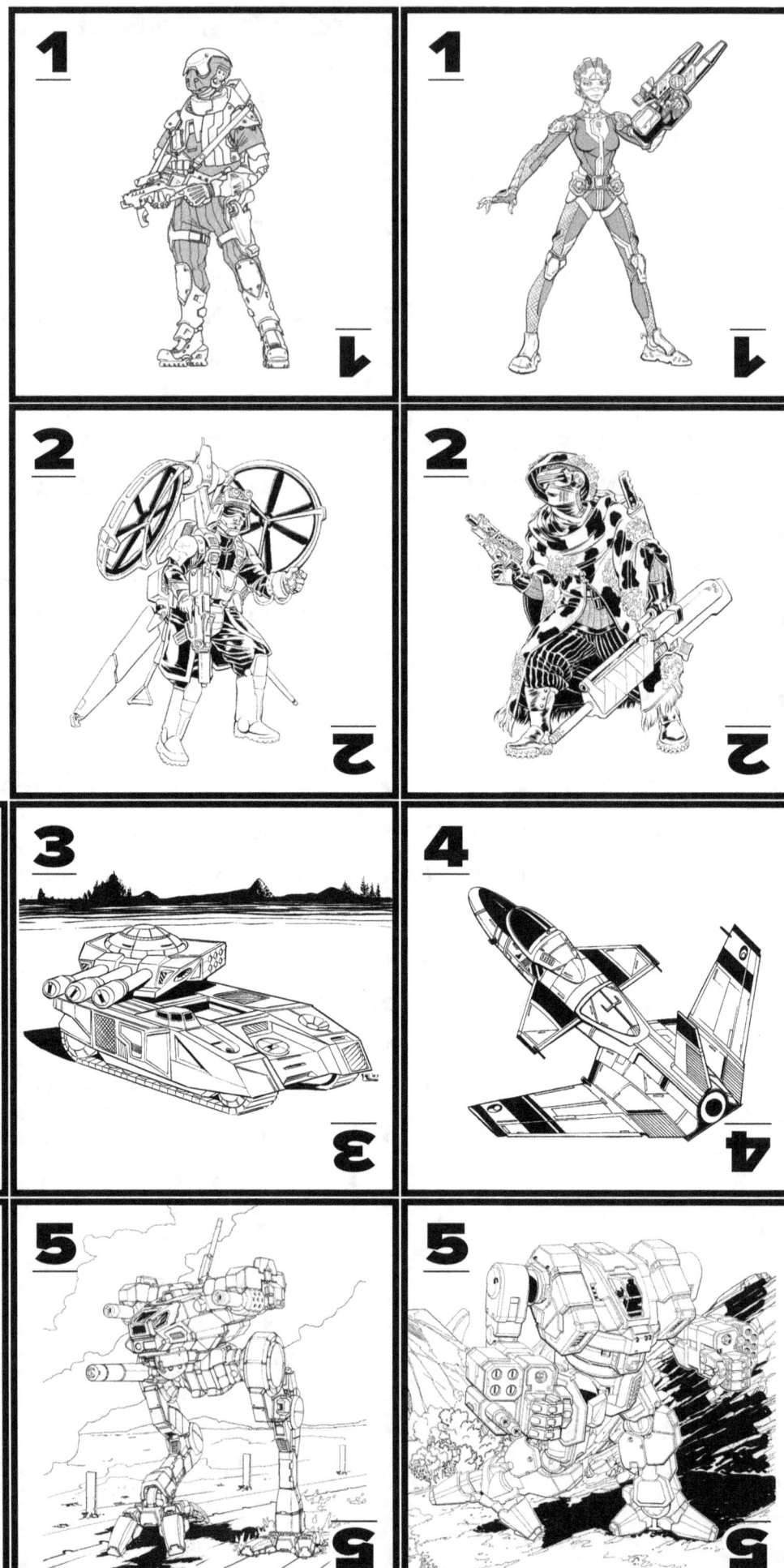

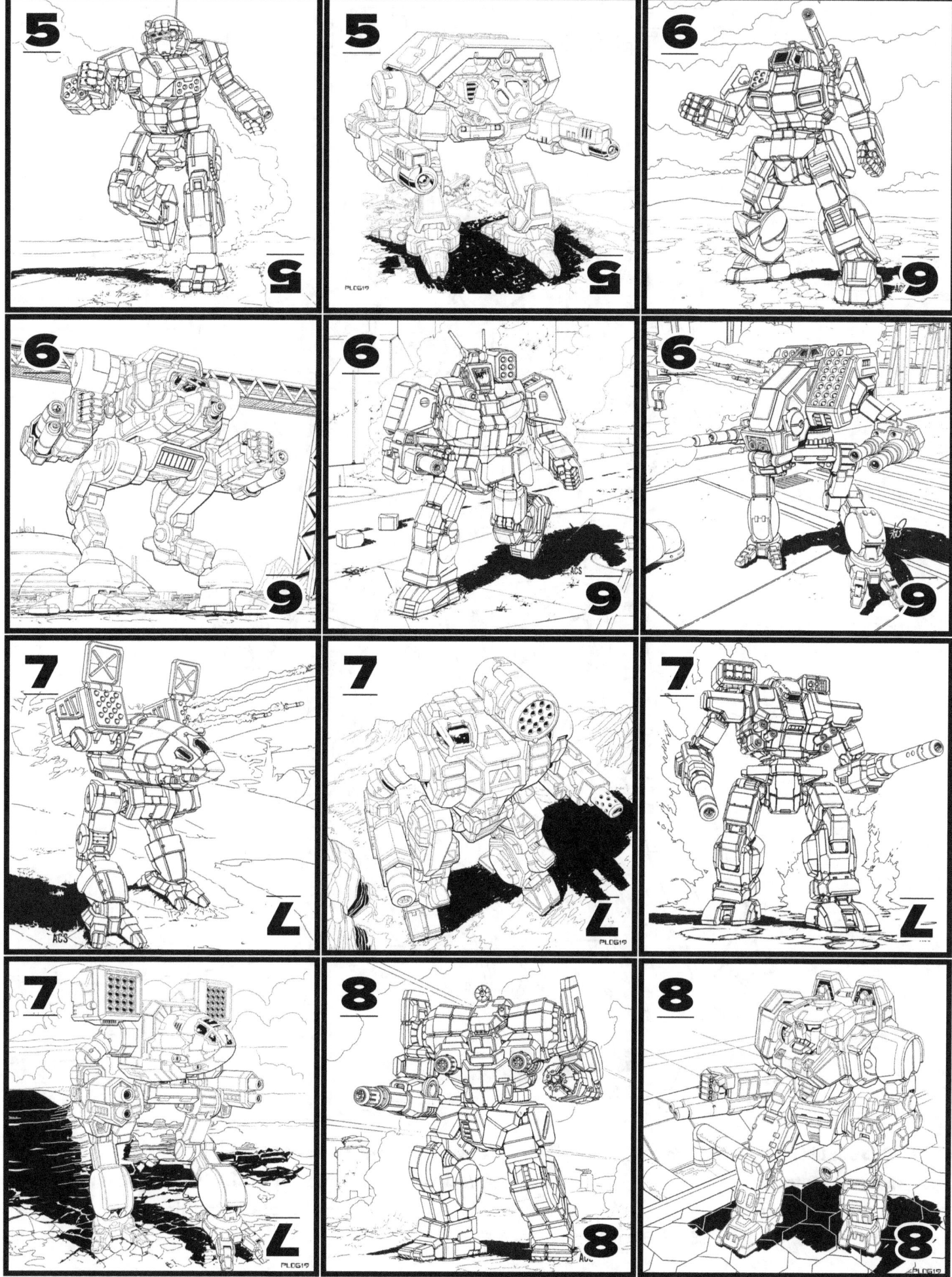

STG-3R STINGER

CLASS: Light BattleMech

MASS: 20 tons

SPEED: 97 kph

JUMP JETS: Chilton 360 (180 m)

ARMOR: 3 tons Riese 100

ARMAMENT: 1 Omicron 3000 Medium Laser
2 LFN Linblad Machine Guns

EXECUTIONER (GLADIATOR)

<PLOG15

CLASS: Assault Clan OmniMech

MASS: 95 tons

SPEED: 86 kph (with MASC)

JUMP JETS: Pryzhok WM 10 (120 m)

ARMOR: 13.5 tons Arcadia Compound Delta VII Ferro-Fibrous

ARMAMENT: 1 Gauss Rifle
2 ER Large Lasers
2 Machine Guns

MAZE

Four Clan MechWarriors want to capture the specs of a new OmniMech configuration at the center of Clan Coyote's vault. They are racing to see who will be able to pilot this dangerous new weapon platform in Operation Revival's first wave!

You can compete with your friends to see who gets through their maze first!
Or time each of your own attempts and see which Clan is fastest.

Seyla!

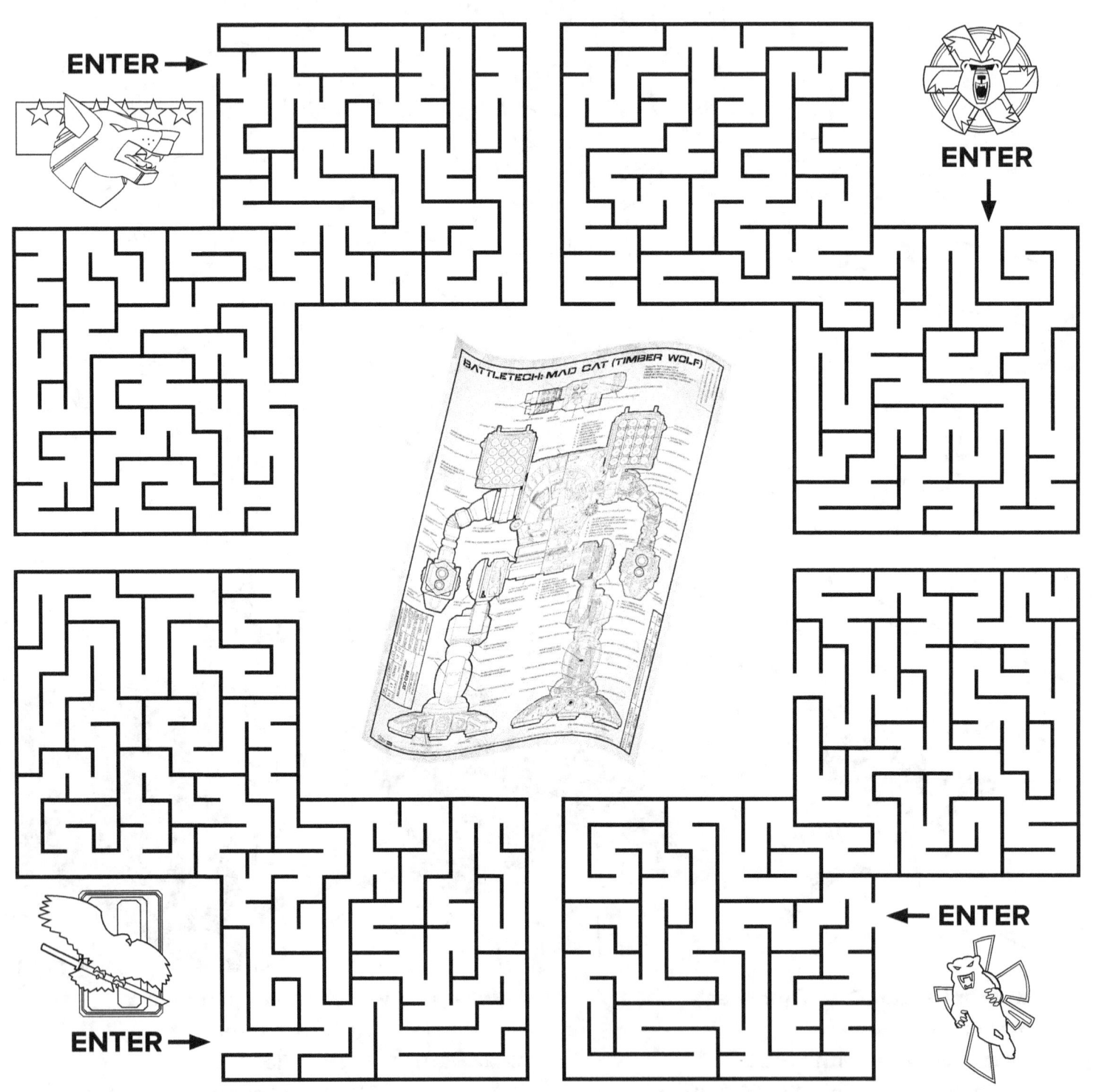

ENTER →

ENTER

ENTER →

← ENTER

TIMBER WOLF (MAD CAT)

PLOG19

CLASS: Heavy Clan OmniMech

MASS: 75 tons

SPEED: 86 kph

JUMP JETS: None

ARMOR: 12 tons Composite A-2 Ferro-Fibrous

ARMAMENT: 2 ER Large Lasers

2 ER Medium Lasers

1 Medium Pulse Laser

2 LRM-20s

2 Machine Guns

VLK-QA VALKYRIE

CLASS: Light BattleMech

MASS: 30 tons

SPEED: 86 kph

JUMP JETS: Norse Industries 3S (150 m)

ARMOR: 6 tons Riese 470

ARMAMENT: 1 Sutel IX Medium Laser
1 Devastator Series-7 LRM-10

WORD SEARCH

CLAN WOLF PERIPHERY TARGETS

- BLACKSTONE
- BUTTE HOLD
- CRELLACOR
- DRASK'S DEN
- FERRIS
- GUSTRELL
- OBERON
- PAULUS
- PLACIDIA
- SIGURD
- THE ROCK

```
A I D I C A L P A C I N C P W F S M F A
Y U O O Y K Z R R B S S D J A D P H X X
B L A C K S T O N E D M K I G U P Q Y U
J R F E I P T X O F Z R G R Y X L G P B
O D P R S B L M S H C K A V E V E U T U
Y Z R P I G E V K U M C M S Y Z N N S T
K E W L I L S J M W K O U A K W Q Q E T
F M R D Z G F I G E M R M Y Y S U Z Q E
L V M I H A C I Y F C E L R W K D S R H
A F C K I U V B B Z K H Y L C P U E B O
G F U W O N J Z B Q L T K R E R H I N L
R Q G W X J B U G F A O E K A R J U J D
J Q A R Q O N Q S V K L W L M C T F E C
O B E R O N Y U K U L B I V Y L P S R P
O O B Q T E A V G A T H M I S Q P W U P
A H M S X B Y H C Q X T Z F I L S X I G
J C I L I S K O X V L N V P G V N R A H
K J W X H W R M J K I V D P U H G Z Z Q
A P S W K Q G R B U R W J L R J J I C W
Q O Q A D L G L D V D B Z Q D Y Z F A Z
```

JADE FALCON 1ST WAVE TARGETS

- ANYWHERE
- BARCELONA
- BONE-NORMAN
- HERE
- PERSISTENCE
- TOLAND
- WINFIELD
- TRELLWAN
- STEELTON

```
D A L M U H J N Q B W U C A E O U H R L
D L H N P D O H A V B V D U W N Y X D F
X L E N C T H R I Z Q Y Y U O Q Q L I C
D O S I L A C E N E U I V X Z V K D M A
H M V E F E D M A J Z O T C H I V C X Y
Y G E L L N N N W H P A C K M P B D X M
B T M O I C I X L I E X G Z P E R K G N
S T N T R L Y W L N Q R Y J U R G B Q N
B A T O L A N D E A A W E O S S Y O G N
A O B C J R R Q R U J Y V K H I F H O K
G D N G X L X E T Q X T F C C S W A I N
H Y L E V R C B Y T X D T M M T D S B V
H Y O T N E N M J O X W R M V E G M P E
L N S H X O X Q P A R G G X T N V D K C
S F D Z Z B R D T O M J T T S C V I M N
R G K U T L W M K D V G B I L E M O E T
A O P O U B B P A E R E H W Y N A O M T
U N D N S E J Q C N F T E V D S F B Q C
Y O J L D I H A T S S O C E A R V A N I
O W K T J N F E Z H G H W C R U Q K F Y
```

COM-2D COMMANDO

CLASS: Light BattleMech
MASS: 35 tons
SPEED: 97 kph
JUMP JETS: None

ARMOR: 4 tons Lexington Limited
ARMAMENT: 1 Shannon Six-Shooter Missile Pack
1 Coventry 4-Tube Missile System
1 Defiance B3M Medium Laser

SUMMONER (THOR)

PLOG19

CLASS: Heavy Clan OmniMech
MASS: 70 tons
SPEED: 86 kph
JUMP JETS: JF Standard (150 m)

ARMOR: 9.5 tons J63-3E Ferro-Fibrous
ARMAMENT: 1 LB 10-X Autocannon
1 LRM-15
1 PPC

ELEMENTALS

CLASS: Clan Battle Armor

MASS: 1000 kg

SPEED: 10 kph

JUMP JETS: Standard (90 m)

ARMOR: 250 kg Standard

ARMAMENT: 1 Detachable SRM-2

1 Modular Weapon Mount
(Small Laser, Flamer, or Machine Gun)

1 Anti-Personnel Weapon Mount

CPLT-C1 CATAPULT

CLASS: Heavy BattleMech

MASS: 65 tons

SPEED: 64 kph

JUMP JETS: Anderson Model 21 (120 m)

ARMOR: 10 tons Durallex Heavy

ARMAMENT: 2 Holly Long Range Missile 15 Packs
4 Martell Medium Lasers

CROSSWORD PUZZLE

CROSSWORD CLUES

ACROSS

5 The Inner Sphere calls it a *Dragonfly*
7 Federated Suns First Prince c. 3025
9 A pilot's ability that helps them aim
11 Kuritan samurai code
12 Legendary *Archer* pilot
14 80-ton Assault 'Mech bristling with PPCs
17 Jungle-hunting feline Clan totem (2 words)
19 Destination of the first SLDF exodus
20 The BattleMech at home in a rainstorm?
21 Legendary Natasha's nickname (2 words)
25 Formerly Clan Sea Fox (2 words)
26 The Usurper of the Star League
29 Clan Invasion's Operation _____
30 AC/10 for example
34 Beowulf would not like this OmniMech
37 Common direct-energy BattleMech weapons
38 Lyran Archon c. 3025
39 BattleMech reactor's power source
40 A Lyran would say "Indomitable _____"
42 Enormous faction that spans the Inner Sphere
   in 3052, informally
43 Missile-boating Capellan BattleMech
44 'Mech muscles
45 Co-developer Clan of the OmniMech with Clan Sea Fox
46 Star League military (abbr.)
47 The Draconis Combine's Great House

DOWN

1 "No _____, no galaxy"
2 CCAF's _____ Commandos
3 Long _____ Missile
4 Free World League's Great House
6 An emerald raptor's invading Clan (2 words)
8 Clan rules of honorable combat
9 A wintery ursine's invading Clan (2 words)
10 Clan Ghost Bear founding couple's surname
13 Young First Lord _____ Cameron
15 First Interstellar Government (2 words)
16 A Kuritan would say "Honor the _____"
18 Clan Nova Cat Khan c. 3052
22 Mortal insult to a trueborn Clanner
23 Common Inner Sphere currency
24 Group that ensures a merc's fair payment. (abbr.)
27 Clan OmniMech that avoids bright light? (2 words)
28 'Mech that could have been called the *Skunk Bear*
31 Wooden 75-ton OmniMech? (2 words)
32 A sacred Clanner's salute
33 A Davion would say "By Freedom's _____"
35 Council of _____ Archons
36 The _____ Creed of Kalvar
41 _____ of Blake
43 Ostensibly neutral faction
46 Capellan Confederation's capital planet

Stumped? Many answers can be found in the *BattleTech: A Game of Armored Combat Primer* or the *Clan Invasion Primer*…but not all of them!

DIRE WOLF (DAISHI)

PLOG19

CLASS: Assault Clan OmniMech
MASS: 100 tons
SPEED: 54 kph
JUMP JETS: None

ARMOR: 19 tons Compound 12B2 Standard
ARMAMENT: 4 ER Large Lasers
    4 Medium Pulse Lasers
    2 Ultra Autocannon/5s
    1 LRM-10

GARGOYLE (MAN O' WAR)

CLASS: Assault Clan OmniMech

MASS: 80 tons

SPEED: 86 kph

JUMP JETS: None

ARMOR: 11 tons Forging C629/j Ferro-Fibrous

ARMAMENT: 1 ER Small Laser

2 LB 5-X Autocannons

2 SRM-6s

MAD DOG (VULTURE)

CLASS: Heavy Clan OmniMech

MASS: 60 tons

SPEED: 86 kph

JUMP JETS: None

ARMOR: 8.5 tons Compound SJ6CW Ferro-Fibrous

ARMAMENT: 2 LRM-20s

2 Medium Pulse Lasers

2 Large Pulse Lasers

HELLBRINGER (LOKI)

CLASS: Heavy Clan OmniMech
MASS: 65 tons
SPEED: 86 kph
JUMP JETS: None
ARMOR: 8 tons Forging Omni-H24

ARMAMENT: 1 ECM
1 Active Probe
1 Targeting Computer
1 Anti-Missile System
2 ER PPCs

4 Anti-Personnel Pods
3 ER Medium Lasers
1 Streak SRM-6
2 Machine Guns

CODE BREAKING

ComStar Adept Sandor Kalman has intercepted coded transmissions!
He's provided you with decoding ciphers—see if you can learn what the secret messages say.

ARC-2R ARCHER

CLASS: Heavy BattleMech
MASS: 70 tons
SPEED: 64 kph
JUMP JETS: None

ARMOR: 13 tons Maximillian 100
ARMAMENT: 4 Diverse Optics Type 18 Medium Lasers
2 Doombud Long Range Missile 20-Racks

WVR-6R WOLVERINE

CLASS: Medium BattleMech
MASS: 55 tons
SPEED: 86 kph
JUMP JETS: Northrup 12000 (150 m)

ARMOR: 9.5 tons Maximillian 60
ARMAMENT: 1 Whirlwind Autocannon
1 Harpoon-6 SRM Launcher
1 Magna Mk II Medium Laser

MAD-3R MARAUDER

CLASS: Heavy BattleMech

MASS: 75 tons

SPEED: 64 kph

JUMP JETS: None

ARMOR: 11.5 tons Valiant Lamellor

ARMAMENT: 2 Magna Hellstar PPCs

2 Magna Mk II Medium Lasers

1 GM Whirlwind Autocannon

MAZE

Lieutenant Lovisa Bjornstrom has uncovered a long-forgotten Star League Fortress and is trying to reach a mothballed WHM-7A *Warhammer*—a "royal" configuration with highly advanced weaponry and systems. Unfortunately the fortress is filled with dead-end corridors and hallways to confound any thieves or spies. Can you guide her to the prize at the center?

Luckily, getting out will be no trouble at all with the firepower of that machine!

ENTER
↓

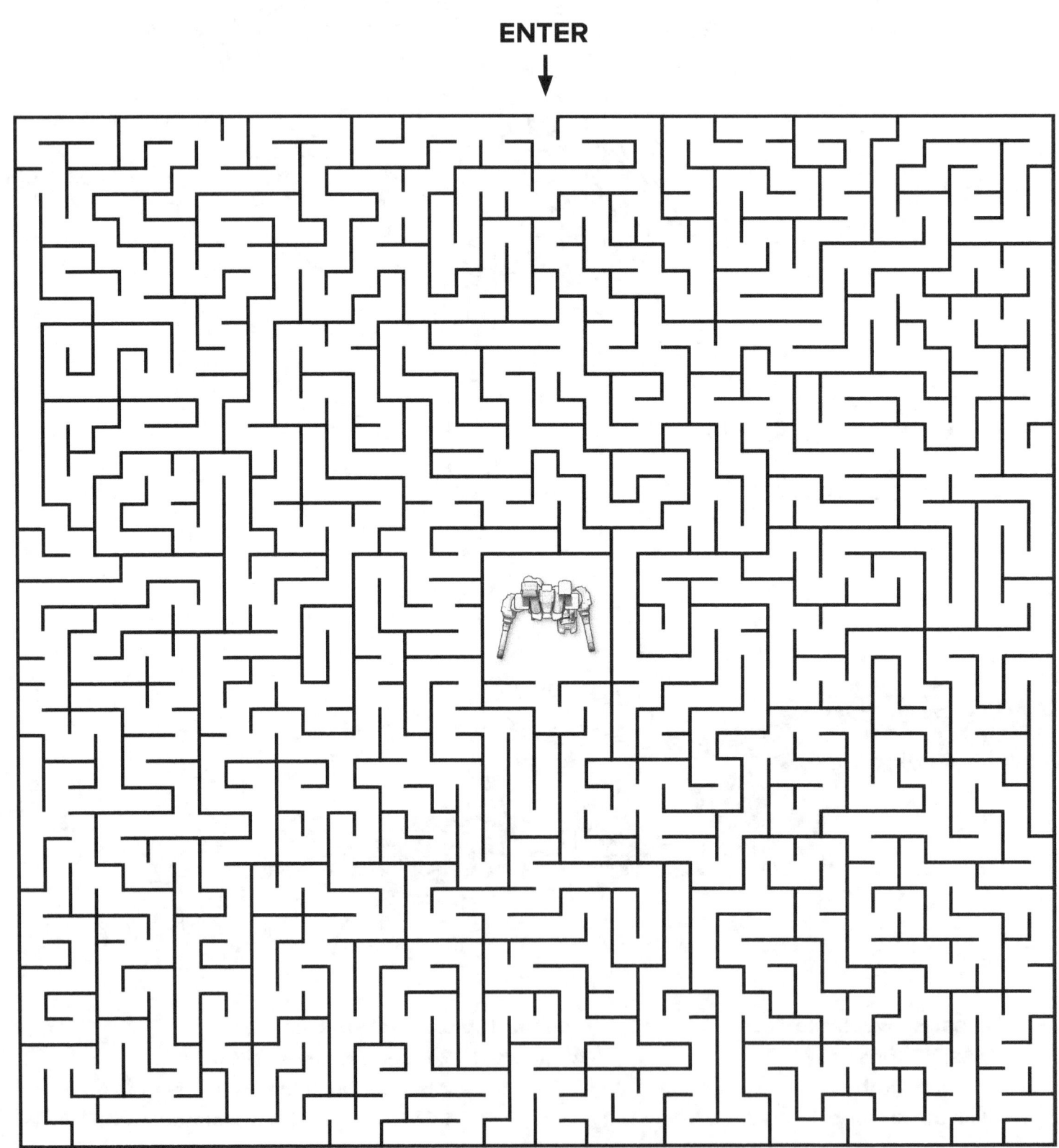

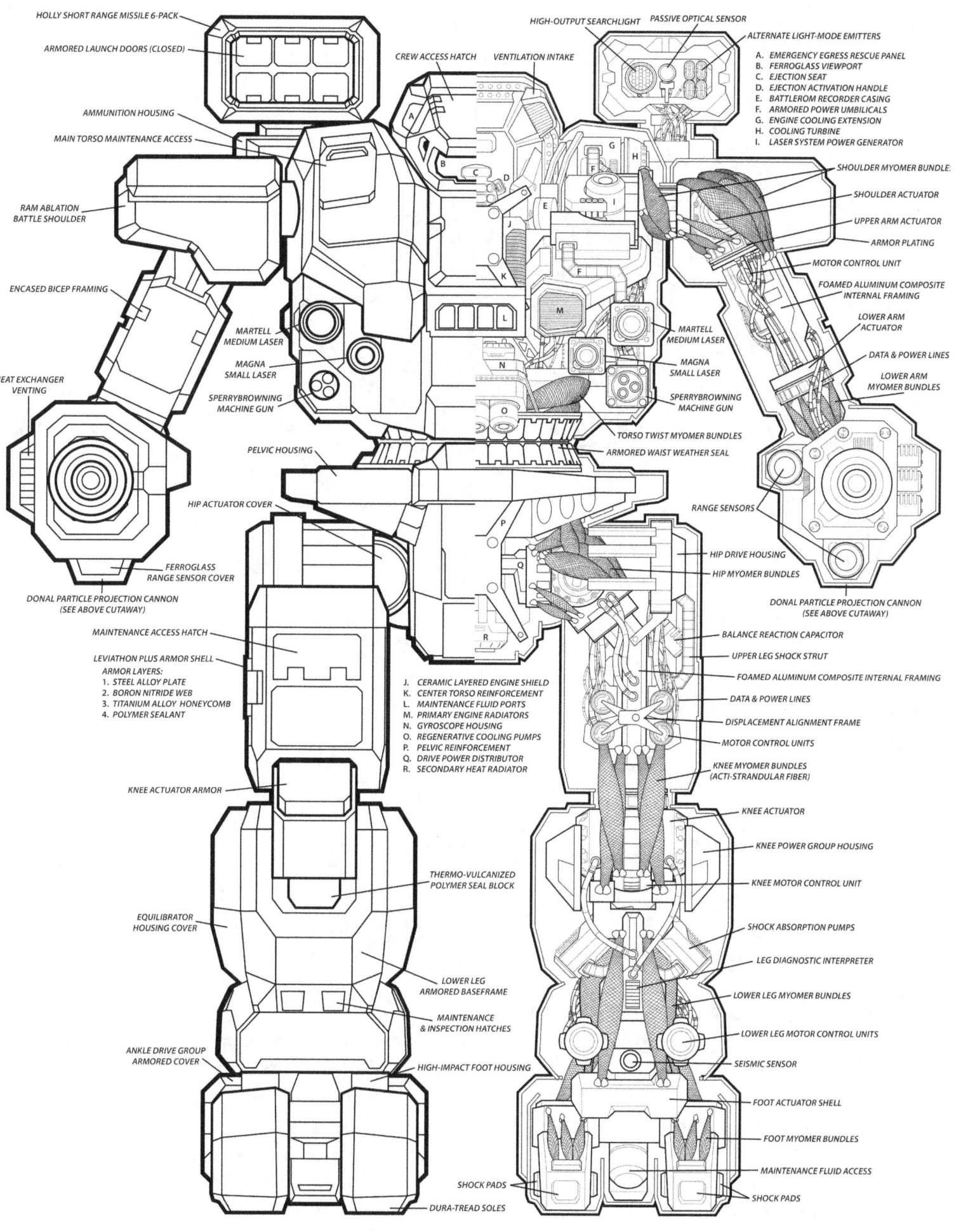

HOLLY SHORT RANGE MISSILE 6-PACK

ARMORED LAUNCH DOORS (CLOSED)

CREW ACCESS HATCH

VENTILATION INTAKE

HIGH-OUTPUT SEARCHLIGHT

PASSIVE OPTICAL SENSOR

ALTERNATE LIGHT-MODE EMITTERS

A. EMERGENCY EGRESS RESCUE PANEL
B. FERROGLASS VIEWPORT
C. EJECTION SEAT
D. EJECTION ACTIVATION HANDLE
E. BATTLEROM RECORDER CASING
F. ARMORED POWER UMBILICALS
G. ENGINE COOLING EXTENSION
H. COOLING TURBINE
I. LASER SYSTEM POWER GENERATOR

AMMUNITION HOUSING

MAIN TORSO MAINTENANCE ACCESS

SHOULDER MYOMER BUNDLE:

SHOULDER ACTUATOR

UPPER ARM ACTUATOR

RAM ABLATION BATTLE SHOULDER

ARMOR PLATING

MOTOR CONTROL UNIT

FOAMED ALUMINUM COMPOSITE INTERNAL FRAMING

ENCASED BICEP FRAMING

LOWER ARM ACTUATOR

DATA & POWER LINES

LOWER ARM MYOMER BUNDLES

HEAT EXCHANGER VENTING

MARTELL MEDIUM LASER

MAGNA SMALL LASER

SPERRYBROWNING MACHINE GUN

MARTELL MEDIUM LASER

MAGNA SMALL LASER

SPERRYBROWNING MACHINE GUN

TORSO TWIST MYOMER BUNDLES

ARMORED WAIST WEATHER SEAL

PELVIC HOUSING

HIP ACTUATOR COVER

RANGE SENSORS

HIP DRIVE HOUSING

HIP MYOMER BUNDLES

FERROGLASS RANGE SENSOR COVER

DONAL PARTICLE PROJECTION CANNON (SEE ABOVE CUTAWAY)

DONAL PARTICLE PROJECTION CANNON (SEE ABOVE CUTAWAY)

BALANCE REACTION CAPACITOR

MAINTENANCE ACCESS HATCH

UPPER LEG SHOCK STRUT

FOAMED ALUMINUM COMPOSITE INTERNAL FRAMING

LEVIATHON PLUS ARMOR SHELL
ARMOR LAYERS:
1. STEEL ALLOY PLATE
2. BORON NITRIDE WEB
3. TITANIUM ALLOY HONEYCOMB
4. POLYMER SEALANT

J. CERAMIC LAYERED ENGINE SHIELD
K. CENTER TORSO REINFORCEMENT
L. MAINTENANCE FLUID PORTS
M. PRIMARY ENGINE RADIATORS
N. GYROSCOPE HOUSING
O. REGENERATIVE COOLING PUMPS
P. PELVIC REINFORCEMENT
Q. DRIVE POWER DISTRIBUTOR
R. SECONDARY HEAT RADIATOR

DATA & POWER LINES

DISPLACEMENT ALIGNMENT FRAME

MOTOR CONTROL UNITS

KNEE MYOMER BUNDLES (ACTI-STRANDULAR FIBER)

KNEE ACTUATOR ARMOR

KNEE ACTUATOR

KNEE POWER GROUP HOUSING

KNEE MOTOR CONTROL UNIT

THERMO-VULCANIZED POLYMER SEAL BLOCK

SHOCK ABSORPTION PUMPS

EQUILIBRATOR HOUSING COVER

LEG DIAGNOSTIC INTERPRETER

LOWER LEG MYOMER BUNDLES

LOWER LEG ARMORED BASEFRAME

MAINTENANCE & INSPECTION HATCHES

LOWER LEG MOTOR CONTROL UNITS

SEISMIC SENSOR

ANKLE DRIVE GROUP ARMORED COVER

HIGH-IMPACT FOOT HOUSING

FOOT ACTUATOR SHELL

FOOT MYOMER BUNDLES

MAINTENANCE FLUID ACCESS

SHOCK PADS

DURA-TREAD SOLES

SHOCK PADS

WHM-6R WARHAMMER

ACS

CLASS: Heavy BattleMech

MASS: 70 tons

SPEED: 64 kph

JUMP JETS: None

ARMOR: 10 tons Leviathon Plus

ARMAMENT: 2 Donal PPCs

2 Martell Medium Lasers

2 Magna Small Lasers

1 Holly Short Range Missile 6 Pack

2 SperryBrowning Machine Guns

UM-R60 URBANMECH

CLASS: Light BattleMech

MASS: 30 tons

SPEED: 32 kph

JUMP JETS: Pitban 6000 (60 m)

ARMOR: 6 tons Durallex Medium

ARMAMENT: 1 Imperator-B Autocannon
1 Harmon Small Laser

CAN YOU DESIGN A NEW OMNIMECH?

The Clans want a new OmniMech design! Can you combine these prototype parts into a versatile 'Mech?

Carefully cut out the parts and assemble them. Glue or tape them together on a fresh sheet of paper.

You can draw your own new parts and add them to the mix, too.

Be sure to name your new war machine!

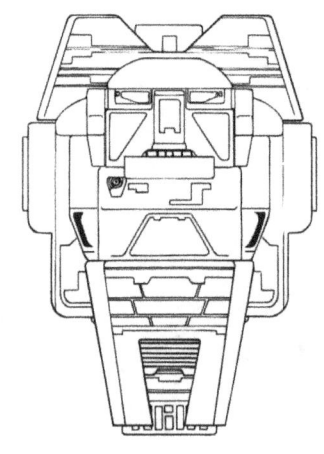
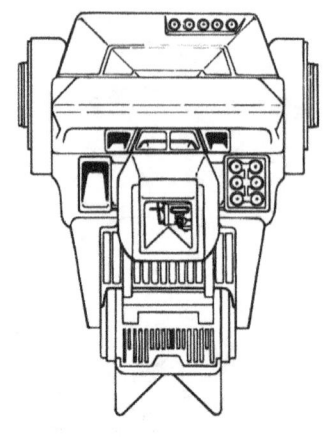
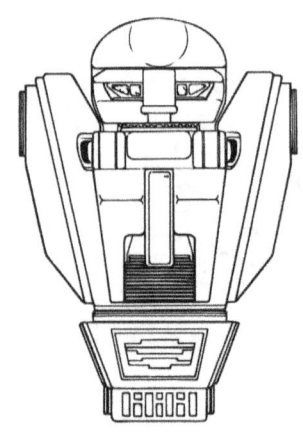

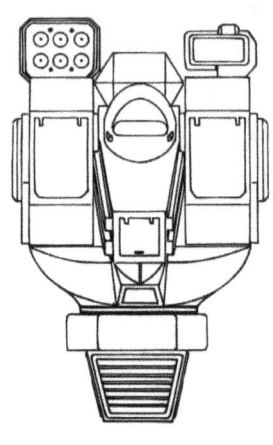
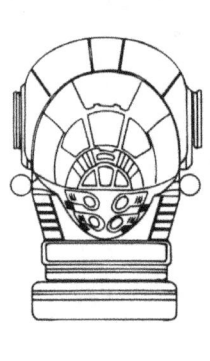
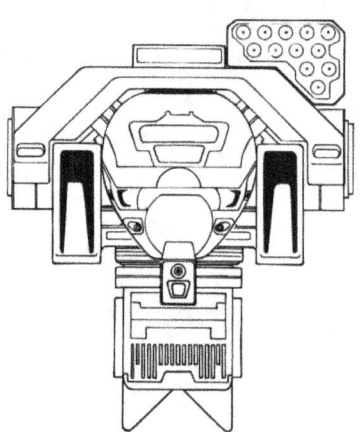

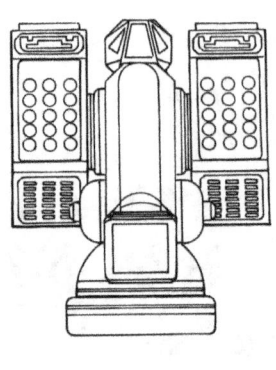
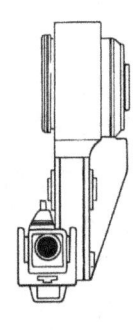
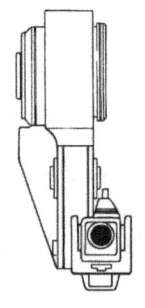
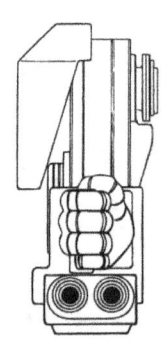
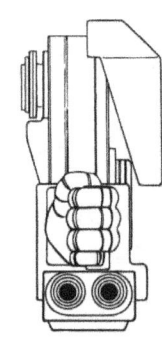

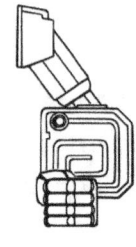
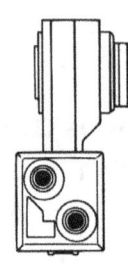
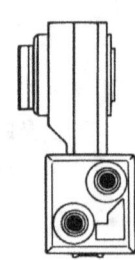
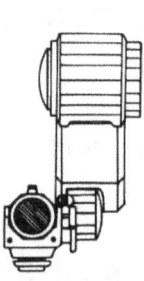
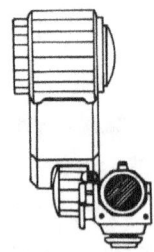

CAN YOU DESIGN A NEW OMNIMECH?

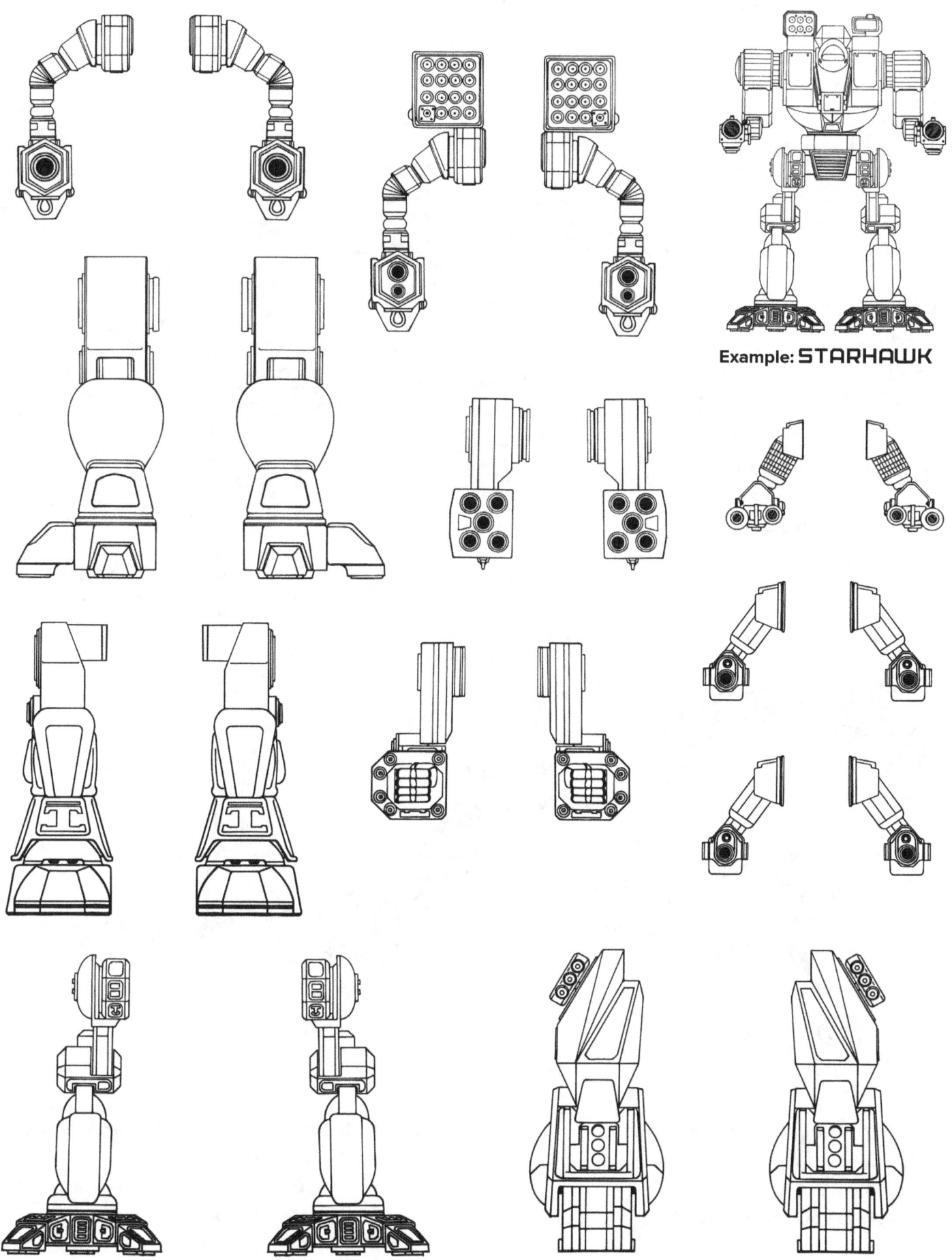

Example: STARHAWK

VIPER (DRAGONFLY)

Class: Medium Clan OmniMech
Mass: 40 tons
Speed: 129 kph
Jump Jets: Geotec 300 (240 m)

Armor: 7 tons Compound H17 Ferro-Fibrous
Armament: 1 SRM-4
　　　　　　1 Anti-Missile System
　　　　　　2 Medium Pulse Lasers
　　　　　　2 Machine Guns

AWS-8Q AWESOME

CLASS: Assault BattleMech

MASS: 80 tons

SPEED: 54 kph

JUMP JETS: None

ARMOR: 15 tons Durallex Heavy Special

ARMAMENT: 3 Kreuss PPCs

1 Diverse Optics Type 10 Small Laser

ICE FERRET (FENRIS)

CLASS: Medium Clan OmniMech

MASS: 45 tons

SPEED: 129 kph

JUMP JETS: None

ARMOR: 7.5 tons MAC Level 5 Ferro-Fibrous

ARMAMENT: 1 Active Probe

1 ER PPC

1 ER Small Laser

1 Streak SRM-2

RESERVE CLAN INSIGNIAS

CLAN NOVA CAT

CLAN DIAMOND SHARK

CLAN STEEL VIPER

CREDITS:

BattleTech
Original Design
   Jordan K. Weisman
   L. Ross Babcock III
   Sam Lewis

BattleTech Line Developer
   Ray Arrastia

BattleTech Art Director
   Anthony Scroggins

Project Development
   David "Dak" Kerber

BattleTech Line Editor
   Aaron Cahall

Writing, Puzzles, Layout
   David "Dak" Kerber

Proofing/Fact-Checking
   Joshua Franklin
   Johannes Heidler
   Philip A. Lee
   Mike Miller
   Eric Salzman
   Chris Wheeler

Illustrations
   Ray Arrastia
   David R. Deitrick
   Brent Evans
   Scott James
   David Kerber
   Chris Lewis
   Matthew Plog
   Anthony Scroggins
   Steve Venters
   Stanley Von Medvey

FIND US ONLINE:

precentor_martial@catalystgamelabs.com
(e-mail address for any BattleTech questions)

http://bg.battletech.com/
(official BattleTech web pages)

http://www.CatalystGameLabs.com
(Catalyst web pages)

http://www.store.catalystgamelabs.com
(online ordering)

Printed in USA.

Published by Catalyst Game Labs,
an imprint of InMediaRes Productions, LLC.
7108 S. Pheasant Ridge Dr.
Spokane, Washington 99224

BG.BATTLETECH.COM